D1391405

characters created by
lauren child

# I really
# ABSOLUTELY
# must have
# glasses

PUFFIN

Text based on the
script written by
Bridget Hurst

Illustrations from the
TV animation produced
by Tiger Aspect

PUFFIN BOOKS
Published by the Penguin Group: London, New York, Australia,
Canada, India, Ireland, New Zealand and South Africa
Penguin Books Ltd, Registered Offices: 80 Strand, London WC2R 0RL, England

puffinbooks.com

This edition published in Great Britain in Puffin Books 2012
001 – 10 9 8 7 6 5 4 3 2 1
Text and illustrations copyright © Lauren Child/Tiger Aspect Productions Limited, 2008
Charlie and Lola word and logo ® and © Lauren Child, 2005
*Charlie and Lola* is produced by Tiger Aspect Productions
All rights reserved
The moral right of the author/illustrator has been asserted
Manufactured in China
ISBN: 978-0-718-19525-0
This edition produced for the Book People Ltd,
Hall Wood Avenue, Haydock, St Helens, WA11 9UL

I have this little sister Lola.
            She is small and very funny.
Lola is thinking about seeing
          because tomorrow Mum is taking her
to the **optician** to have her **eyes** tested.

Lola says,
"But my eyes do not need testing, Charlie."

So I say,
"But going to the optician's is fun.

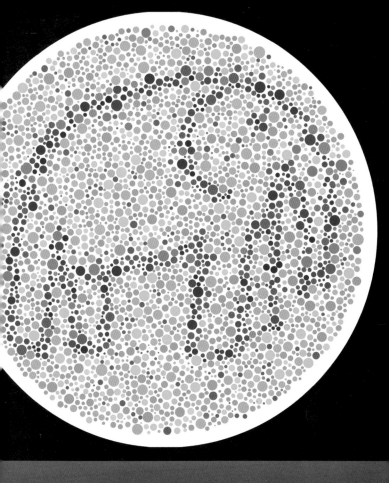

You get to find hidden pictures
        in lots and lots of coloured dots."

And Lola says,
        "Dots, Charlie? I love dots!"

Lola says,
"I can actually see very well.
I can see my spaghetti, and my bowl,
and my spoon,
and my pink milk.

AND I can see YOU!

So I really absolutely do not
need to have an **eye** test."

At school,
Lola says, "Look! Mini's got glasses!"

So Lotta asks Mini,
"Where did you get your glasses?"

And Lola says,
"They are especially very nice and flowery!"

And Mini says, "I went to the Optician.
          She said that I need glasses because
everything I see is slightly fuzzy."

Later on, Lola says,
        "Charlie, I can't wait to go
to the **eye** tester!
    I am going to get some flowery **glasses**."

So I say,
"Lola, you'll only get **glasses** if you
really, really need them."

And Lola says,
"But I DO really need them...

"... because I cannot see that pink biscuit...

and I cannot see my yellow toothbrush...

and now I can
definitely not see at all."

So I say, "That's because it is dark."

And Lola says,
"Oh, yes! But when I get my new glasses,
I'll be able to see in the dark."

I say, "No you won't, Lola."

But Lola says, "I will, Charlie! I will!"

The next day,
Lola asks Mini,
"Can I try on your glasses?"

But Mini says,
    "The **optician** lady told me
it's not a good idea because
    everyone's **eyes** are different.
My **glasses** might make your **eyes** a bit achy."

So Lola asks,
"But how will I know which
**glasses** will look nice on me?"

Mini says,
    "Oh, that's easy. At the **optician's**, you try on lots of **glasses** to see what you like best!"

And Lola shouts,
        "I can't wait! I can't wait!"

Later, Lola and I go to the **optician's**.

Lola looks at all the
different **glasses**.

When it's her turn to see the **optician**,
    Lola says,
    "See you later, Charlie...
        with my **glasses**!"

On the way home, Lola says,
"The **Optician** said I absolutely
do not need **glasses**, Charlie."

So I say, "That's good!
It means your **eyes** are very strong."

And Lola says,
"But I really, really wanted glasses."

Then I say,
"I have an idea!"

Lola and I cut, paste and colour
pieces of paper.

We sprinkle **glitter**, stick on **sparkly** stars
and add **squiggly** lines
until we make...

the absolutely most PERFECT
pair of **glasses**.

At school, Lola wears her new **glasses.**
Lotta has made some, too!

Mini says, "I like your **glasses,** Lola."

And Lola says,
"Yes, **glasses** can be fun
even if you don't need them!"